TWENTY YAWNS

by Jane Smiley · illustrated by Lauren Castillo

two lions

TO VERONICA—J.S
FOR NOAH, ADAM, ALISON, AND MATT—L.C.

Published by Two Lions, New York
www.apub.com

Amazon, the Amazon logo, and Two Lions are
trademarks of Amazon.com, Inc., or its affiliates.

ISBN-13: 9781477826355 (hardcover)
ISBN-10: 1477826351 (hardcover)
ISBN-13: 9781477830680 (paperback)
ISBN-10: 1477830685 (paperback)

Library of Congress Control Number: 2014915910

Design by Sara Gillingham Studio
The artwork was created digitally with painted textures.

Printed in Mexico

First Edition

two lions

The beach umbrella was
flapping in the breeze.

flap!

Flap,

Flap,

flap!

Not far from the waves, Lucy
was digging a hole all by herself.

It got so big that her dad could lie down in it. When he did, she covered him up. They laughed and laughed.

Then he took her hand, and they ran
into the water. A big wave came in,
and he swung her into the sky.

Lucy walked with Mom and Dad

all the way to the end of the beach.

On the way back, Lucy rolled and
rolled down the soft warm dunes.

Even though she got dizzy and sandy,
she didn't want to stop.

Mom and Dad and Lucy stayed longer at the beach than they ever had before.

Lucy **YAWNED.**
Mom **YAWNED.**
Dad **YAWNED.**

Mom said, "Early bedtime!"

Outside Lucy's bedroom, the sun
was sinking below the horizon.
Strips of clouds were pink and red.

Lucy put her pajamas on inside out,
climbed into bed, and yawned a big

YAWN.

Mom began to read her a story. "Once upon a time, there lived a wonderful little boy named Fred. He was perfect in every way, or so his mother said." Lucy stretched and smiled.

She gave a big big big YAWN

and closed her eyes.

Mom stopped reading. She was asleep!

The moon shone through the window,
a silver veil that fell across the floor.
Everything looked mysterious, even
Lucy's own hands on the bedspread.
Suddenly, Lucy was wide awake.

She looked around. Everyone in the pictures seemed to be watching her—Grandma, Grandpa, Aunt Elizabeth, Mom, and Dad.

Even Fred, in the book that Mom had dropped on the floor.

Lucy slipped out of bed and padded to the door.
Her dad was snoring in the living room.

...ZZZZz

The house was **verrrrry** quiet.
Lucy needed Molasses, her bear.

He was wedged beneath
Hornet the giraffe,
Juno the horse,
Mathilda the alligator,
Frank the kangaroo,
and his baby, Leonard.

SWOOSh!

All the toys fell to the floor.

Lucy started to carry Molasses back to her bed. But the other toys were looking at her, even Leonard, the baby kangaroo. They seemed lonely.

So one by one,
she brought them
over to her bed
and dropped
them in a patch
of moonlight.

She spread her blankie over them and kissed them good night. Now they looked sleepy and happy.

Lucy lay down and snuggled
in next to her friends,
sighed a big happy sigh, and

YAWNED.

She saw Grandma
YAWN.

She saw Grandpa
YAWN.

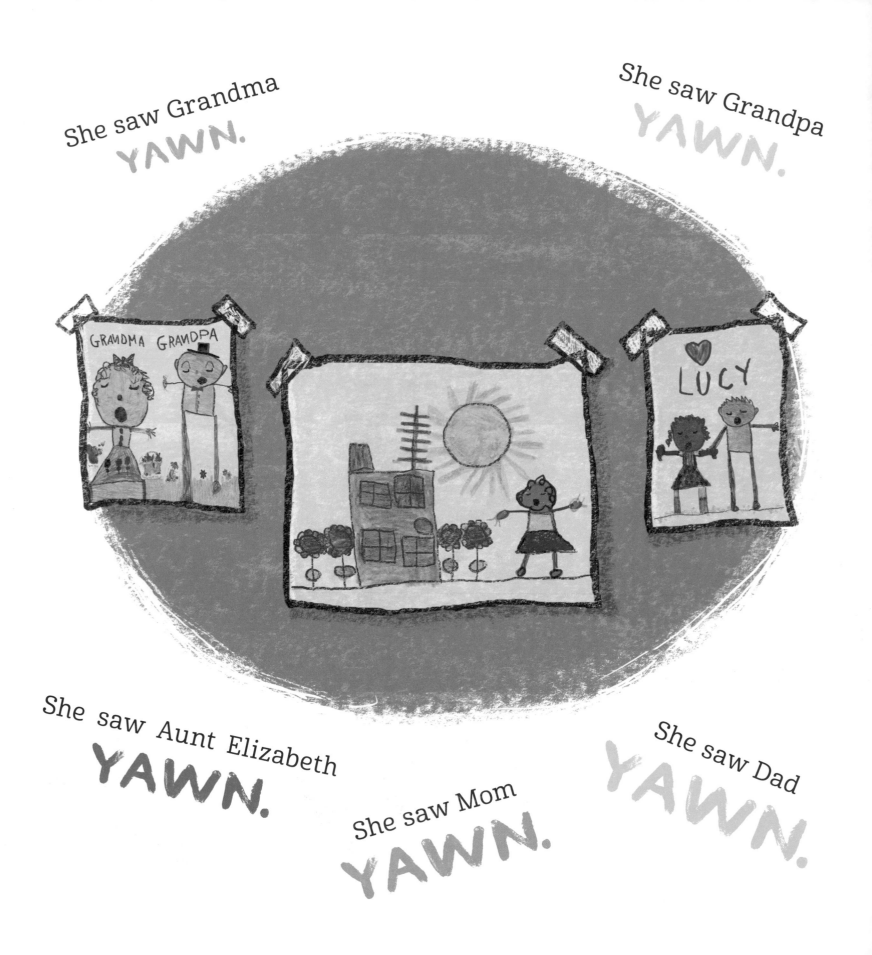

She saw Aunt Elizabeth
YAWN.

She saw Mom
YAWN.

She saw Dad
YAWN.

She saw Fred,
the boy in the book,
YAWN.

She saw the moon
YAWN.

Lucy put her arms around Molasses. He seemed especially tired. Then she gave one last

YAWN . . . and fell asleep.